Sherman the Sheep

by Kevin Kiser
illustrated by Rowan Barnes-Murphy

Macmillan Publishing Company   New York   Maxwell Macmillan Canada   Toronto
Maxwell Macmillan International   New York   Oxford   Singapore   Sydney

Library of Congress Cataloging-in-Publication Data
Kiser, Kevin. Sherman the sheep / by Kevin Kiser ; illustrated by Rowan Barnes-Murphy. — 1st ed.   p.   cm.
Summary: A flock of adventurous sheep learn that, after all, home is best. ISBN 0-02-750825-0   [1. Sheep—Fiction.]
I. Barnes-Murphy, Rowan, ill.   II. Title. PZ7.K644Sh 1994   [E]—dc20   92-22745

To my wife, SuAnn, who might quite possibly be even smarter than Sherman! —K.K.

For Paige Gillies —R.B.-M.

One day Sherman the Sheep was napping beneath his favorite apple tree when his cousin Wayne trotted up.

"Wake up, Cousin Sherman!" said Wayne.

Sherman opened one eye. "What is it, Wayne?" he asked.

"Sherman," said Wayne, "the flock is not happy with this field anymore. We want to live in the best field in the valley and we want you to lead us there."

Sherman sighed and said, "Why me?"

"Everyone knows you are the smartest sheep in the field," said Wayne. "Maybe even in the whole valley!"

"Baaa…" said Sherman modestly. "I don't know about that,

but I do know where the best field in the whole valley is."

"Let's go!" said Wayne.

"It's a long, hard journey," Sherman said, "but if it's what you all want, follow me."

As Sherman led the flock out of the field, he made up a song and the flock sang along:

"We're sheep! We're sheep!
We're brave and we're bold,
We go where we want,
And not where we're told,
'Cause we're sheep! We're sheep!"

After a while Wayne said, "Are we almost there, Sherman? We're hungry!"

"Perhaps this sign will tell us where we can find food," said Sherman.

"I didn't know you could read signs, Sherman!" said Wayne.

"Sign reading is a bit of an art," said Sherman. He tilted his head and closed one eye. The whole flock was quiet while Sherman studied the sign. "I believe this sign says FREE FOOD FOR SHEEP," said Sherman. He led the flock down the side road.

"This grass tastes like spinach!" Wayne whined.

"Never mind," said Sherman. "The grass is always sweet in the best field in the valley."

On the road again, Sherman sang a song and the flock sang along:

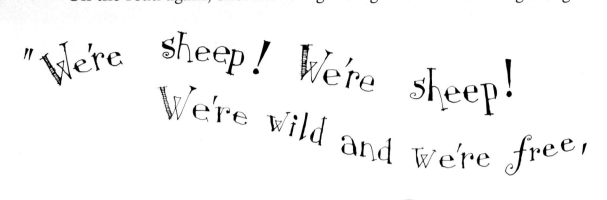

"We're sheep! We're sheep!
We're wild and we're free,

We see what we like,
and we like what we see,
'Cause we're sheep! We're sheep!"

Soon it began to rain. "Are we almost there, Sherman?" asked Wayne. "We hate getting wet!"

"No problem," said Sherman. "I think this sign says SHELTER FOR SHEEP."

"Look!" said Sherman. "A barn with wheels!" He led the flock into the strange barn. Suddenly the barn began to move, slowly at first, then faster and faster.

"This barn makes me dizzy!" wailed Wayne.

"Don't worry," said Sherman. "The barn never moves an inch in the best field in the valley."

Finally the rain stopped falling and the barn stopped moving.

On the road again, Sherman sang a song and the flock sang along:

"We're sheep! We're sheep!
We're fast and we're strong,
Wherever we go,

The sun came out again and soon it was very hot.
"Are we almost there, Sherman?" asked Wayne.
"We're thirsty!"

"If I am not mistaken, this sign says HEY, SHEEP,
WATER AHEAD," said Sherman. "Look, there is
even a drinking platform!"

Sherman led the flock onto the platform.

"This water tastes like mud!" Wayne sputtered.

"No matter," said Sherman. "The water is always
fresh and clear in the best field in the valley."

STOP
AHEAD
FERRY CROSSING

On the road again, Sherman sang a song and the flock sang along:

"We're sheep! We're sheep!
We're clever and smart,

We always finish
Whatever we start,
'Cause we're sheep! We're sheep!"

They marched down long, dusty roads. They scrambled up steep, winding paths. They pranced across high, shaky bridges. Finally Sherman stopped at the top of a hill and said, "We're here!"

The flock crowded forward and looked down at the best field in the whole valley. "Ohhh!" they said, and "Ahhh!"

"I do believe this sign says SHEEP ARE HAPPY HERE," said Sherman.

As Sherman led the flock into the field, he sang a song and the flock sang along:

"We're sheep! We're sheep!
We're happy to say,
We've found the best field,
And we're home to stay,
'Cause we're sheep! We're sheep!"

"Sherman, this field looks very familiar," said Wayne. "Isn't this our old field?"

"Of course!" said Sherman. "Our field has always been the best field in the valley. I wouldn't live anywhere else."

"You really are the smartest sheep in the valley," said Wayne. "Maybe even in the whole world!"

"Baaa…" said Sherman modestly. Then he yawned and settled down beneath his favorite apple tree to finish his nap.